SACRAMENTO PUBLIC LIBRARY

D0468259

SACRA

SACRAMENTO, CA 95814

6/2008

Ni i ko i cè kanyi su fé, ni dugu jèra i na yé.

If you say you are beautiful at night,
when daylight comes you will be seen.

This book is dedicated to my
grandmother, Sabou Diakité,
from whom I heard my first stories.

The proverb and the songs in the story are in Bambara, which is
spoken by six million people in Mali.

Copyright © 2007 by Baba Wagué Diakité

All rights reserved. No part of this publication may be
reproduced, stored in a retrieval system or transmitted, in any
form or by any means, without the prior written consent of the
publisher or a license from The Canadian Copyright Licensing
Agency (Access Copyright). For an Access Copyright license, visit
www.accesscopyright.ca or call toll free to 1-800-893-5777.

Groundwood Books / House of Anansi Press
110 Spadina Avenue, Suite 801, Toronto, Ontario M5V 2K4
Distributed in the USA by Publishers Group West
1700 Fourth Street, Berkeley, CA 94710

Library and Archives Canada Cataloging in Publication
Diakité, Baba Wagué
Mee-an and the magic serpent : a folktale from Mali / Baba Wagué
Diakité.
ISBN-13: 978-0-88899-719-7
ISBN-10: 0-88899-719-1
1. Folklore–Mali. I. Title.
PZ8.1.D564Me 2006   j398.2'096623   C2006-904740-5

Design by Michael Solomon
Printed and bound in China

Mee-An and the Magic Serpent

Baba Wagué Diakité

A Folktale from Mali

GROUNDWOOD BOOKS
HOUSE OF ANANSI PRESS
TORONTO   BERKELEY

On the edge of the desert a beautiful but vain young girl named Mee-An lived with her parents and her magical younger sister, Assa.

Mee-An was looking for a perfect husband. She could not bear the thought of a man who bore a single scratch, scar or blemish on any part of his body.

"I am so beautiful, I deserve someone as perfect as I am," she told her sister.

Suitors seeking Mee-An's hand in marriage came from far and wide offering her parents cola nuts. But as soon as Mee-An saw them she rejected them all, finding fault in even the tiniest blemish.

"Seeing a person is not the same as knowing him," Mee-An's mother cautioned.

But stubborn Mee-An would not listen.

Assa, Mee-An's sister, was younger but she was wiser. She was tired of all the hapless suitors, so one day she decided to help find the perfect man. She turned herself into a fly and went off to the marketplace in search of a man without a single scratch, scar or blemish on any part of his body. Whenever she spotted a newcomer in the village, she would fly all around him, landing annoyingly here and there. But she could not find a perfect man anywhere.

The young men in the village knew all about Mee-An and her hopeless quest. They whispered about her amongst themselves. Her fame spread far and wide.

One day two young shepherds who lived quite far from the village sat down in the shade of a giant termite hill. They started to talk about their favorite subject – Mee-An and how no man was good enough for her. Little did they know that a powerful serpent had made his home in this exact same termite hill.

When the magic serpent overheard their conversation, he became very excited. He decided to turn himself into a perfect young man in order to win this beautiful girl.

Disguised as a handsome young man, the magic serpent arrived in the village to discover a big celebration in progress. People were drumming and dancing in the marketplace.

As usual, Assa was busily buzzing around inspecting the strangers who had come for the party. She quickly noticed the new face of a very handsome young man.

"Ah," she said to herself, "maybe he is the one, at last." And she buzzed and landed and buzzed all around him once more. She could not see a single scratch, scar or blemish on any part of his body. She flew home as fast as she could go.

"Mee-An, I've found him," she said, turning back into a girl. "He is perfect. But there is something very odd about him. He does not smell like a human."

But Mee-An didn't care. "Invite him to come to the house for dinner," she ordered Assa. Then she rushed off to get ready to greet him.

That very same evening the perfect young man, who was really a serpent, arrived at Mee-An's house. While the sisters were cooking, strange things began to happen. First the walls cracked. Cooking pots fell and broke. The wind howled and birds sang wildly.

Mee-An's mother was worried. "These are very bad signs," she whispered to her daughter. "Beware."

But Mee-An turned away and paid no attention to her mother's words of caution.

A month later Mee-An and the magic serpent were married.

When it was time for Mee-An to go to her new home with her perfect new husband, Assa was sent along to act as the *konyo-wuluni*, "the little barking dog of the wedding," as tradition required.

The couple and Assa had to walk for many days, feeling their way through dark forests and crossing large dry deserts before they reached their new home. It was a single hut that stood on the far bank of a great river.

"How will we get to our new house?" asked Mee-An.

"Don't worry," said her husband. "I have a boat. I will get you across."

The sisters had never been so far from their parents.

Despite the strangeness, life soon settled into a routine. The perfect bridegroom went out on the river every day and returned with many fish for their dinner.

Assa had given up her disguise as a fly, but she still loved going out every day, exploring the world along the banks of the river. She found many plants and animals that were new to her.

As for Mee-An, she was so content that she felt herself putting down roots like a tree.

"I will be here forever," she thought happily.

One day the sisters decided to surprise Mee-An's husband on the river by taking him some lunch. They walked a long way. Assa wondered why she had never seen him during her explorations.

After they had walked and walked they heard a strange sound. Peeking through the bushes they saw a giant serpent in the middle of the river. It was singing.

Ne na komo, kô di Mee-An ma,
Mee-An n'a dogo muso ma,
Olu ko dun ku tolo
Ne kolu dun ka untolo nari.

I like to fish for Mee-An,
For Mee-An and her sister,
To fatten them up
So they can make a delicious meal.

The sisters, hearing this terrifying song, suddenly realized that the perfect bridegroom was none other than this very same serpent.

They crept back along the river taking care to hide in the bushes.

"We must go home to our parents," they whispered to each other. "But how will we ever cross the river?"

Suddenly a shadow passed over them. They looked up and saw Balakononifin, the black heron, flying overhead. Assa had seen him before, but he had never spoken to her – even when she had called out to him.

"Please, Balakononifin, help us cross this river. We will be eaten if we don't escape."

But the bird, pausing in his flight, called down to them, "Humans can never be trusted. I cannot help you."

The sisters began to sing this song:

N' tiguè, n' tiguè,
Balakononifin kan kalama jan,
Sô bè n' fè so,
Balakononifin kan kalama jan,
Misi bè n' fè so,
Balakononifin kan kalama jan,
Fali bè n' fè so,
Balakononifin kan kalama jan,
Saga bè n' fè so,
Balakononifin kan kalama jan.
N'olu dima dè,
Balakononifin kan kalama jan.

Take us over, take us over,
O black heron of the river,
I promise you that horse
   I left back home,
O black heron of the river,
I promise you that cow
   I left back home,
O black heron of the river,
I promise you that donkey
   I left back home,
O black heron of the river,
I promise you that sheep
   I left back home,
O black heron of the river,
I will give them all to you,
O black heron of the river.

The heron splashed down into the river beside them.

"Pretty words do not always tell the truth," he said. "If I help, you must keep your promises."

The sisters promised they would keep their word and scrambled up onto his back. Up he flew.

Just as he was crossing the river, the magic serpent saw what was happening. He cleverly sang the same song as the two sisters – but even more sweetly – trying to convince the bird to come back.

But Balakononifin was no fool. He recognized the singer as the very same serpent who stole all the fish from the river. He did not slow in his flight.

The magic serpent was furious to see his beautiful dinner disappearing. High in the air he swirled, wiggling and twisting. The ashes and dust from the ground whirled up with him, caught in his funnel. But even as he twisted and twirled around Balakononifin and the sisters, they flew on. He had no power. He was mere dust.

He fell back into the river, defeated. And ever since, serpents live in the water.

As for Balakononifin and the sisters, they flew home to the girls' family. But the black heron was no longer black. The serpent's dust had turned him white.

Assa and Mee-An kept their promise to the bird. He left with a horse, a cow, a donkey and a sheep. So, to this day, when you see these animals standing by an African river, you will probably also see a white bird proudly seated on their backs.

The sisters soon returned to their old lives. Assa often buzzed into the village to see what was happening close up.

As for Mee-An, she had finally learned that seeing a person is not the same as knowing them. And when she met the man who became her husband, she was able to love him despite his scratches, scars and blemishes.